Karen's Twin

Stephanie Slavcio (handwritten, inverted)

**Look for these
and other books about Karen
in the
Baby-sitters Little Sister series:**

Little Sister

Karen's Twin
Ann M. Martin

Illustrations by Susan Tang

A
LITTLE APPLE
PAPERBACK

SCHOLASTIC INC.
New York Toronto London Auckland Sydney

ISBN 0-590-47044-2

12 11 10 9 8 7 6 5 4 3 2 1   4 5 6 7 8/9

Printed in the U.S.A.   40

First Scholastic printing, January 1994

*This book is for a gigundoly wonderful
pair of twins,
Andrew and Patrick Fulton.*

Families

"Good morning, girls and boys," said my teacher.

"Good morning, Ms. Colman," we replied.

It was the beginning of a new day of school. It was the beginning of a new week of school, too. Monday morning. Some kids do not like school. So they do not like Monday mornings very much. But I love school. (So Mondays are fine.)

I am Karen Brewer. I am seven years old. I wear glasses. I even have two pairs. The blue pair is for reading. The pink pair is for everything else. Also, I have blonde hair, blue eyes, and some freckles. Ms. Colman is my wonderful teacher. She is the best teacher I have ever had, and I am already in the second grade. She is patient, she listens to her students, and she hardly ever yells. If I get a little bit noisy in school, she just says to me, "Indoor voice, Karen."

My school is called Stoneybrook Academy. I am lucky because my two best friends go to Stoneybrook Academy, too. *And* they are in Ms. Colman's class. Their names are Nancy Dawes and Hannie Papadakis. We call ourselves the Three Musketeers. The only bad thing is that we cannot sit together in the back of the classroom anymore. Ms. Colman made me move to the front row after I got those glasses. Now Hannie and Nancy sit in back, and I sit in front with the other glasses-wearers. Guess what. Ms. Colman wears glasses, too.

"Karen," said Ms. Colman that morning.

"Would you please take attendance today?" She handed me her book.

Taking attendance is very cool. You get to stand by Ms. Colman's desk with her book and a pencil, and make check marks. I looked around the room. There were Nancy and Hannie. Check, check. There were Ricky Torres and Natalie Springer. Check, check. They are the other glasses-wearers. Also, Ricky is my pretend husband. We held a wedding on the playground one afternoon. There was Addie Sydney. Check. She rolled into the room in her wheelchair. There was Pamela Harding, my best enemy. Check. There was Audrey Green. Check. I like Audrey because she is almost always nice to everyone, so everyone is nice back to her. She does not have a single enemy. (I wish I could be like Audrey.) There were the twins, Terri and Tammy Barkan. Check, check. Terri and Tammy are identical twins, but my friends and I can usually tell them apart. Anyway, they do not dress alike. And there were

3

Bobby and Hank and Chris and all the other kids. No one was absent that day.

After I had finished taking attendance, Ms. Colman said, "Boys and girls, soon we will begin learning about families. We will learn about our own families and families in other countries. We will even learn about animal families. And we will work with Mr. Berger's class." (Mr. Berger's class is next to ours. Our rooms are connected by a door. You do not have to go into the hallway to get to Mr. Berger's.) "So you might work in Mr. Berger's room," Ms. Colman went on. "Or some of Mr. Berger's students might work in here. Just every now and then. I think you will like the change." Ms. Colman paused. Then she said, "One of our projects will be family trees. Who knows what a family tree is?"

I shot my hand in the air. I happen to know a lot about families. I think I might be an expert on them.

Karen's Family Trees

Guess what. When we make family trees in school, I will have to make two of them. That is because I have two families. Honest. I would have to draw one picture of Mommy's family and another picture of Daddy's family. (That is what a family tree is — a drawing that shows who is in your family and how they are related to each other.)

I did not always have two families, though. When I was very little I had just one family — Mommy, Daddy, Andrew, me. Andrew is my little brother. He is four now, going on five. We lived together in a big house. It was the house Daddy had grown up in. But after awhile Mommy and Daddy said they were going to get a divorce. They had been fighting all the time, and they decided they did not love each other anymore. (They loved Andrew and me very much, though.) The divorce meant they would not live together anymore, either. So Daddy stayed in his house, and Mommy moved into a smaller one. The houses are here in Stoneybrook, Connect-icut. Now Andrew and I live in both houses. We live with Daddy every other weekend and on some vacations and holi-days. We live with Mommy the rest of the time. Lately I have been missing Daddy. I do not think I see him nearly enough. Two weekends a month. That's nothing.

Mommy and Daddy have each gotten married again, but not to each other. Mommy married a man named Seth. He is my stepfather. Daddy married a woman named Elizabeth. She is my stepmother. And that is how Andrew and I got two families.

This is my little-house family: Mommy, Seth, Andrew, me, Rocky, Midgie, and Emily Junior. Rocky and Midgie are Seth's cat and dog. Emily Junior is my pet rat.

This is my big-house family: Daddy, Elizabeth, Kristy, Charlie, Sam, David Michael, Emily Michelle, Nannie, Andrew, me, Boo-Boo, Shannon, Goldfishie, and Crystal Light the Second. Kristy, Charlie, Sam, and David Michael are Elizabeth's kids. (She was married once before she married Daddy.) So they are my stepsister and stepbrothers. Kristy is thirteen. She is a very good baby-sitter. And an even better big sister. I love her very much. Charlie and Sam are old. They go to high school. David Michael is seven like me. But he goes to a different school. Emily Michelle is my adopted sister. She is two and a half. Daddy and Elizabeth adopted her from the faraway country of Vietnam. Nannie is Elizabeth's mother. That makes her my stepgrand-mother. She helps Daddy and Elizabeth run the family. Then there are the pets. Boo-Boo is Daddy's fat old cat. Shannon is David Michael's huge puppy. Guess what Goldfishie and Crystal Light are. (Andrew named Goldfishie, in case you could not tell.)

Since my brother and I have two of so many things, I call us Andrew Two-Two and Karen Two-Two. (I thought of those names after Ms. Colman read a book to my class. The book was called *Jacob Two-Two Meets the Hooded Fang*.) Andrew and I are two-twos because we have two homes and two families, two mommies and two dad-dies, two cats and two dogs. Also we have clothes and books and toys at each house. (This is so we do not have to pack much when we go back and forth.) Plus, I have my two best friends. (Nancy lives next door to Mommy's house. Hannie lives across the street from Daddy and one house down.) I even have those two pairs of glasses.

The only bad thing about being a two-two is that I do not get to see Daddy and my big-house family often enough. Still, I am lucky to be part of two families who love me.

Keep Out, Emily!

Andrew and I go to the big house late on Friday afternoons. Usually, Mommy drops us off just before dinnertime. The first thing I always have to do is hug everybody. Then I have to make sure I find the pets and greet them, too. (The only pet I hug is Shannon. Boo-Boo sometimes puts his claws out, and it is hard to hug goldfish.)

"Hi, Daddy! Hi, Elizabeth! Hi, Kristy! Hi, everybody!" I cried.

Andrew and I had arrived at the big

house. I was ready for the weekend. And I was gigundoly happy to see my family.

Emily Michelle ran to me. She threw her arms around my legs.

"Hug!" she said happily.

I hugged her back. Then I said, "Come with me, Emily. Help me find Shannon and Boo-Boo. Let's go on a pet hunt."

Emily followed me from room to room. "Here, Shannon! Here, Boo-Boo!" I called. "Come say hi!"

"Here, Boo-Boo!" repeated Emily. (She cannot say "Shannon" very well yet.)

When I found Shannon, I hugged her and kissed her. So did Emily.

When I found Boo-Boo, I said, "Hi, Boo-Boo."

Emily said, "Hi, Boo-Boo."

Then I tiptoed into the playroom. I looked in the goldfish tank. "Hi, fish," I said. "How are you doing?"

"Hi, fish," repeated Emily.

At dinner that night, Emily wanted me

to sit next to her. So I changed places with Nannie. I sat beside Emily's high chair. After dinner, Emily followed me into the family room. "Read," she said. She handed me a book. I read her the story. Then I read her two more stories. Each time I finished, she said, "Read."

Finally I said, "Emily, I am tired of reading."

Then Emily followed me to my room. But luckily, Kristy put her to bed.

Guess what woke me up the next morning. Emily. She was jumping on my bed. "Hi, Karen!" she said when I opened my eyes.

I groaned. "Ohhh." Then I said, "Emily, I wanted to sleep late."

"Play," replied Emily.

"No," I said, but I got up anyway.

After breakfast, Hannie came over. We played dress-ups in the playroom. "I hope Emily will not bother us," I said.

Emily did not bother us. She left us alone. But when we went to my room later, Emily was already there. She had been taking things out of my drawers. (Emily likes to open drawers.)

"Emily!" I shrieked. "Go away!" Emily ran out of my room. "She is such a pest," I said to Hannie. "Here, help me with something."

Hannie and I found a box of crayons. On a big piece of pink paper we wrote "KEEP OUT EMILY." I taped the paper to my door. Then I closed the door. "There," I said. "That should do it."

A few minutes later, Kristy knocked at my door. "What is going on?" she wanted to know. "Why is Emily crying?"

"Because I told her to get out of my room," I replied. "She is being a pest. She was looking through my stuff."

"She *likes* you, Karen," said Kristy. "You are her big sister."

"She is still a pest."

"All little sisters are pests," said Hannie. She should know. She has a little sister, too.

"You are my little sister," Kristy said to me. "You are not a pest. Just try to be nice to Emily."

"Okay," I replied. But I left the sign up (even though Emily cannot read).

Twins

A week went by. I was looking forward to Monday. I knew it would be a good day. In school we were going to begin our unit on families. Also, I was wearing a new outfit. Mommy had bought it for me — black leggings and a long sweater with a taxicab on it. I thought the sweater was cool.

That morning Ms. Colman said to my classmates and me, "Boys and girls, what is a family?"

Audrey shot her hand in the air. When Ms. Colman called on her, she said, "It's a mother and a father and children. And maybe some pets. And they all live together."

Ms. Colman did not say whether Audrey was right or wrong. Instead she asked, "Any other ideas? Do you all have families like that?"

"I do," said Bobby Gianelli.

"Me too," said Pamela Harding.

"Not me," said Hank. "I live with my dad and my stepmother. I visit my mother a lot, but I do not live with her."

Tammy raised her hand. "Terri and I live with our parents and our brothers *and* our grandparents," she said. Then she added, "Guess what. Our grandma is a twin, too. An identical twin. Just like Terri and me. Only her sister is not alive anymore."

"A twin grandmother?" said Addie. "Cool."

"*Very* cool," said Audrey.

"I just live with my parents," spoke up Natalie. "I do not have any brothers or sisters."

"I feel like I don't either," said Audrey.

17

"My big brother went away to college. I miss him."

Ricky leaned over and tapped me with his pencil. "Tell about your families, Karen," he whispered.

So I raised my hand. "I live with more than one family," I said. "I live with two. Mommy's family and Daddy's family. All together, I have a mother, a father, a stepmother, a stepfather, a stepgrandmother, a brother, three stepbrothers, a stepsister, and an adopted sister. Oh, and two dogs, two cats, two goldfish, and a rat."

Most kids in my class already knew this. A few did not. One of them was Chris Lamar. His mouth dropped open. "Boy," he said.

On the playground that day, Nancy and Hannie and I played hopscotch. We needed to jump around to stay warm. The weather was freezing. I was glad I was wearing leggings — and a sweater underneath my jacket. I rubbed my hands together while I waited for my turn.

18

"Hi, Karen," said Audrey. She watched Hannie hop to home and turn around.

"Hi," I replied. "Want to play?"

"Sure," said Audrey. She pulled a rock out of her pocket. Then we both watched Nancy. She was taking a long turn. "You know what?" asked Audrey. "I think you have the most interesting family in our class, Karen. And I have the most boring."

"Your family is not boring," I told her.

"I think it is. My brother is never even home anymore. I wish I had a sister. Or a *twin* sister. Wouldn't that be cool? I would always have someone to play with. Like Terri and Tammy."

"I guess," I replied. I was still watching Nancy. She had just thrown her rock and missed. It was my turn.

"Karen?" said Audrey. "Would you be my twin?"

I tossed out my rock. "Sure," I replied as I hopped away. I was hoping I could catch up with Nancy.

Just Like You

I forgot that Audrey had asked me to be her twin. I was busy playing hopscotch. (Hannie won the game.) Then I was busy in school. Then I was busy at Nancy's house after school. Then I was busy at the little house. I did not think about twins again until the next day.

On Tuesday I went to school wearing jeans and a red sweater.

Guess what Audrey wore. She came into our classroom wearing black leggings and a long sweater with a taxicab on the front.

It was exactly like my new outfit.

"Hi, Karen," she said. "How do you like it? I asked my parents if they could buy it, and they said yes."

"That's great," I replied.

"I know. Now we are twins."

I looked down at my jeans and the red sweater. "Well, not really," I said. "We are not even dressed the same."

"But we *could* be dressed the same," said Audrey.

While we waited for Ms. Colman to arrive, I sat in the back of the room with Hannie and Nancy. Audrey sat with us. I perched on a desk and crossed my right leg over my left. Audrey perched on a desk and crossed her legs the same way.

In gym class that day, Audrey was the captain of the Blue Team. "I want Karen on my team!" said Audrey. "I call Karen!"

I smiled. That was nice. I am not always called first.

At lunch, Audrey said, "Karen! Sit with me!" (Hannie and Nancy and I all sat with her.) Audrey watched me eat my lunch. She ate hers in the same order. Apple first, then sandwich, then raisins. (Only Audrey did not have raisins. She ate chips while I ate my raisins.)

"Boy, am I hot," I said later. I pushed up the sleeves of my sweater.

"Boy, so am I," said Audrey. She pushed up the sleeves of her sweater.

On the playground Audrey said, "Let's play follow-the-leader. Then I can do just what Karen is doing."

Before we went inside that day, Audrey said, "Pssst, Karen. Here is a piece of candy for you. A Tootsie Roll. I have one, too. Since we are twins."

"Candy? Thanks!" I said. "I like being your twin, Audrey."

I knew we were not really twins, but so what? This was a good game. Audrey had chosen me to be on her team. She had

asked me to sit with her at lunch. And now she had given me candy.

"What are you eating, Karen?" Nancy asked as we entered Ms. Colman's room. "You have chocolate breath."

"A Tootsie Roll," I replied. "Audrey gave it to me."

"Why?" asked Nancy.

I shrugged. "Because she is nice, I guess."

"Does she have any more candy?" Hannie wanted to know.

"I will ask her," I replied. I tapped Audrey on the shoulder. "Do you have any more Tootsie Rolls?" I said. "Nancy and Hannie want some, too. I do not want to eat in front of them."

"Sorry," replied Audrey. "I just had two. One for me and one for my twin." She grinned at me. Then she followed me to my desk. "Here," she said. "Write with this pencil this afternoon. It is the same as mine." Audrey handed me a brand-new pencil.

"Thanks!" I exclaimed.

"You're welcome. Isn't this fun? I am just like you. Oh, Karen, wear your taxi sweater to school tomorrow, okay?"

I nodded. It was nice that Audrey wanted to be just like me.

Emily's Papers

I could not wait for my next weekend at the big house. It is just not fair that I can only see Daddy two times a month. That is not often enough. I tried to be patient, but I do not think I was. Neither was Andrew. He wanted to see Daddy, too. He kept saying to Mommy, "How many more days till we go to Daddy's?"

But when we finally went back to the big house, something was wrong. The moment I walked through the front door, I got a funny feeling. First of all, when Andrew and I ran inside, David Michael was the only person there to greet us.

"Where is everybody?" I asked.

"Charlie and Sam are still at school," he replied. "And Kristy is baby-sitting." Then he leaned close to us. "Everyone else is looking for something," he whispered.

"What are they looking for?" I whispered back.

"Papers. Emily's papers."

I did not know what David Michael was talking about. I put down my knapsack. Then I peered into the living room. Nannie was there. She was looking through a desk. All the drawers were open. Papers spilled out of them and onto the floor.

"Go look in the TV room," David Michael whispered to me.

I looked. Daddy was in there, going through another desk. Then I found Elizabeth in the kitchen. She had taken every paper out of the desk by the telephone.

David Michael and I shrugged at each other.

Grown-ups.

At dinnertime, the adults were in very bad moods. They snapped at each other. When Elizabeth said, "Is there any more salad?" Nannie replied, "No, there is not. I forgot to make enough for an army."

I decided not to ask if Nannie had made dessert.

That night, Kristy put me to bed. "What is wrong with everyone?" I asked her. "The grown-ups are acting very strange."

"There is some problem with Emily's adoption papers," Kristy replied.

"Oh," I said. I knew that Daddy and Elizabeth had had to fill out lots and lots of forms, and sign lots and lots of papers so they could adopt Emily. Daddy kept calling the papers "red tape." I did not know why. I had not seen a speck of tape, red or any other color. I also knew that Daddy and Elizabeth had not quite finished with the papers. Emily was not quite finished being adopted yet. But she was going to be soon. And then we were going to have a big party to celebrate Adoption Day.

"Is it a bad problem?" I asked Kristy.

"I'm not sure," she replied. "But do not worry about it, Karen."

After Kristy left my room I could not fall asleep. I heard Daddy and Nannie come upstairs. They were talking in quiet, angry voices. Then Nannie went downstairs, and Daddy got on the telephone. Later Elizabeth got on the telephone. She made call after call. Two were to Peter Lambert. He is a lawyer.

I kept getting up for drinks of water. Then I kept getting up to go to the bathroom. One time I heard Daddy say to Elizabeth, "Ask Peter if we can file late. They did not send us what we need. They did not send us the proper document. That was not our fault. They cannot hold us responsible. That is not fair to us or to Emily."

I wondered what would happen if the grown-ups had a big problem with Emily's papers. Emily would not have to go back to Vietnam, would she?

I began to feel afraid. And guilty. When I told Emily to get out, I did not mean it. I did not hope it would *really* happen.

Karen's Twin

On Saturday, Daddy and Elizabeth and Nannie were still making phone calls and looking at papers. But they did not seem so upset. And nobody had packed a suitcase for Emily.

On Sunday, Andrew and I went back to the little house. I hated to say good-bye to my big-house family, especially Daddy. But I had to. That is the way things are for a two-two.

On Sunday night, Audrey called me.

"Hi, Karen," she said. "How is my twin?"

I smiled. "I'm fine."

"What are you wearing to school tomorrow?" Audrey wanted to know. "Have you decided yet?"

"Yup," I replied. I had just laid out my clothes. I knew exactly what I was going to wear. "My jeans skirt," I told Audrey, "a white turtleneck shirt, a yellow sweater, white tights, and my red shoes. Why?"

"Oh, I just wondered."

The next morning, Nancy and I went to school together. Nancy's father drove us. When we reached our classroom, Audrey was already there. And this is what she was wearing: a jeans skirt, a white turtleneck shirt, a yellow sweater, white tights, and red shoes. Her outfit was not exactly the same as mine, because her shoes were different and so was her sweater. But it was close.

"Hey!" exclaimed Nancy when she saw Audrey. "You and Karen are twins! Cool."

32

Audrey pulled me aside. "You forgot to wear your taxi sweater last week after I told you to. So I thought I would find out what you were going to wear. Then I could dress just like you."

I was glad that Audrey still wanted to be just like me. It was a nice feeling. Sometimes I want to be just like Kristy. That is because I think she is gigundoly wonderful.

"Hey, look! The Bobbsey Twins!" said Chris, when he saw Audrey and me.

"Yeah, twins!" echoed Leslie Morris.

Audrey just grinned.

That night, Audrey called me again.

"What are you wearing tomorrow?" she asked.

I thought of the clothes I had laid on my chair. "My blue dress and red hair ribbons and the red shoes again," I said.

"Which blue dress?" asked Audrey.

"The striped one with the long sleeves."

"Okay. 'Bye, twin!"

" 'Bye, Audrey."

On Tuesday, Audrey wore a blue striped

dress with short sleeves. It was not the same as mine. But it was close.

"The twins are back," said Pamela.

"Yup," I said. I blew my bangs out of my face.

"Yup," said Audrey. She blew at her hair, too. "Being a twin is gigundoly fun, isn't it, Karen?"

"Gigundoly," I agreed.

"Well, my goodness," said Ms. Colman as she hurried into our room. "How will I tell everyone apart today?"

I looked around. I saw Audrey and me in our matching outfits. Then I saw Terri and Tammy. They were wearing matching outfits, too. They *never* dress the same. I could hardly tell which one was Terri and which one was Tammy. We were having a twin time in Ms. Colman's room. (I was glad Ms. Colman wouldn't *really* have trouble telling Audrey and me apart.)

Audrey's Glasses

On Friday, Audrey said to me, "Karen? Can you come over and play at my house tomorrow? My parents said you can stay for lunch."

"I have to ask Mommy," I replied. (I remembered to add, "Thank you.")

Mommy said I could play at Audrey's. She drove me to her house just before lunchtime. Of course, Audrey had called me the night before. This time she had said, "Wear the outfit with the taxi sweater. Then we can look exactly alike."

So I did.

"Hi! Hi, twin!" cried Audrey when she opened her front door. Audrey was jumping around. "We are going to have a great day! I fixed our lunch myself! I fixed peanut butter and honey sandwiches and apple slices and cookies. Oh, and we rented *The Little Mermaid*! And we are allowed to eat in front of the TV!"

"It sounds as if you are going to have a fun afternoon, Karen," said Mommy. "Seth will pick you up at five, okay?"

"Okay," I replied. Then we called good-bye to each other.

Audrey pulled me inside. She led me into the TV room. A table had been set in front of the TV. (Well, not *right* in front of it, but near it.) She served us our lunch. Then she switched on *The Little Mermaid*.

I had seen that movie five or six times already. I love the story of Ariel. So I was happy to watch it again.

Audrey and I sat down side by side at the table. I picked up my sandwich. Audrey

36

picked up hers. I crossed my feet. Audrey crossed hers. I nibbled at my crusts. Audrey nibbled at hers. Then I smiled at Audrey and she smiled at me.

The movie went on. I ate my apple slices. Audrey ate hers. I ate my cookies. Audrey ate hers. Once I tried to trick Audrey. I reached for a cookie, but then I switched and picked up an apple slice instead. Audrey copied me exactly.

The thing about being a twin that was not fun was being watched. Audrey watched me all the time so she could copy me. She was always looking at me.

When the movie was over, we cleared away our dishes. Then we sat at the table and colored pictures. Audrey drew whatever I drew. After awhile I wanted to put my hand over my paper so Audrey could not see what I was making. But I thought that might be rude. Besides, Audrey said, "Karen, you make the best pictures. I want to draw just like you."

"Thank you," I replied politely.

Soon I ran out of things to color.

"I have an idea," said Audrey. She jumped up. She began to look through a box of dress-up clothes. "Look what I have!" she exclaimed. Audrey held up an old pair of blue glasses. Actually, they were just the frames. They looked a little like my reading glasses. "I *thought* these were in here," said Audrey as she put them on. She sounded triumphant. "Now I look even more like you."

Audrey pulled me into the bathroom. She was still wearing the fake blue glasses. She studied us in the mirror. "Hmm. Our hair does not look much alike," she said. (That is true. For one thing, Audrey's hair is brown.)

"You know what?" said Audrey. "I need bangs like yours, Karen. Would you give me bangs?"

"You want me to cut your hair?" I cried.

"Oh, no. Sorry." I have gotten in enough trouble cutting my own hair. I was not going to cut someone else's. "I cannot do that, Audrey," I said.

I was not sure I liked being a twin after all.

Terri and Tammy

Audrey did not seem upset when I said I would not cut her hair. We just played dress-ups until Seth came to take me home.

On Sunday night, Audrey called to find out what I was wearing to school the next day. On Monday we both wore blue jeans and our taxi sweaters. Also, Audrey wore the blue glasses. And she had bangs. Someone had cut her hair.

Terri and Tammy came to school wearing matching dresses. "My goodness," said

Ms. Colman again when she saw the four of us.

That morning we worked on our family projects some more. We had been working on them for awhile. Every morning we would divide into two groups. Half of us would go to Mr. Berger's room, and the rest of us would stay with Ms. Colman. Then half of Mr. Berger's students would come into our room. I was with the group that stayed in our own classroom. So was Audrey. And so was Nancy. But Hannie went to Mr. Berger's room. Audrey said she was glad she was in the same group as her twin. She felt sorry for Terri and Tammy. That was because they could not be together. Terri went to Mr. Berger's room. Tammy stayed in Ms. Colman's room.

The kids in Ms. Colman's room had been working on their family trees. Like I said, I needed two trees — one for a picture of Mommy's family, one for a picture of Daddy's family. Daddy's family tree was enormous. It was gigundo. At first I had gotten confused and didn't know where to stop drawing. I made boxes for Daddy and Andrew and Emily and me, and wrote our names inside the boxes. Then I made boxes for Elizabeth and her kids. And Nannie. Then I wondered if I should add Elizabeth's first husband, since he is the father of Kristy and my stepbrothers. That was when I got confused. Ms. Colman told me to stick with Daddy's part of the family. She said it would be easier. Even so, I erased a lot when I was working on the tree. Finally, I had to start it over again. I was still finishing it that day when Ms. Colman began to talk about animal families. I drew boxes and wrote names and colored leaves on the tree while I listened to Ms. Colman. I wanted both of my trees to be perfect.

Twin Day

Audrey still called me every night to find out what I was going to wear to school. And I always told her. I felt funny when Audrey did everything I did — when she copied me and wore fake glasses and cut her bangs — but I was not angry at Audrey. She was always nice to me. Still, sometimes I wanted to play just with Hannie and Nancy. I did not want to play with Audrey every single minute.

Then one day in school Audrey pulled me and Tammy and Terri aside.

"Guess what," she said. "I have decided to have Twin Day, and you are all invited. It will be next Saturday."

"What is Twin Day?" asked Tammy.

"It is just for twins," Audrey replied. "That is why you and Terri are invited. So are my friends Marilyn and Carolyn Arnold. They are twins who do not go to our school. And of course Karen is coming because she is my twin. Three sets of twins."

"Cool," said Terri and Tammy.

"Yeah, cool," I echoed, even though I was not sure. Audrey and I would be the only ones who were not *really* twins.

On Twin Day, Mommy picked up Tammy and Terri. She drove the three of us to Audrey's house. Marilyn and Carolyn had already arrived. (I know the Arnold twins a little bit. Kristy and her friends baby-sit for them pretty often.)

"Who wants to see *Aladdin*?" Audrey's mother asked us. "Today we will go out to lunch, and then go to the movies."

"Really?" I cried. Maybe Twin Day would be okay after all.

When Mommy left, Audrey's parents helped Audrey, me, Terri, Tammy, Marilyn, and Carolyn into a van. They drove us downtown. First we went to the Rosebud Cafe. I just love that place. It has good food plus lots of ice cream sodas and sundaes.

We sat in the back. We took up one long table. All the twins sat next to each other — Terry and Tammy, Marilyn and Carolyn, and Audrey and me in our taxi sweaters.

"Well, look at this!" exclaimed the waitress when she brought our menus. "*Two* sets of twins. Imagine that."

Audrey gave her the evil eye, but she did not say anything. I knew she was mad, though. And I wanted her to feel better. "It must be our glasses," I whispered to Audrey. "I have to wear my pink ones, and you only have blue ones."

46

Later, a man at the table next to ours leaned over. He said to Audrey's parents, "It isn't every day you see *two* sets of twins. I thought I had double-double vision!"

"Hmmphh," grumped Audrey. "Let's take off our glasses, Karen."

I shook my head. "Nope. I am not allowed to. Besides, I would not be able to see. Sorry."

When we went to the movie theater the ticket-taker grinned. *"Two* pairs of twins!" he exclaimed. "This must be my lucky day!"

"Hey! What about *us*?" cried Audrey. She pointed to me, then to herself.

"Oh, nice sweaters," said the man.

"But — but — " Audrey did not know what to say.

I pushed her forward. "Come on. Everyone is waiting for us."

Mrs. Green bought a bucket of popcorn. Then we found eight seats together. A kid in front of us said, "Look, Dad! Four twins! Cool!"

Audrey slumped down in her seat. She stayed that way during the whole movie. She could not have seen much. I said, "Audrey, watch the movie. It is very funny."

But all she would reply was, "No. Everyone is stupid."

The Great Idea

After Twin Day, Audrey was in a bad mood until Tuesday. She would not talk to anyone. Then she cheered up. She turned into regular old Audrey. Regular Audrey who was nice to everybody. On Tuesday night she called to find out about my outfit. On Wednesday we were twins again.

Something else happened on Wednesday. We had divided into our two groups. Ms. Colman was standing in front of the classroom.

"Boys and girls," she said, "Mr. Berger and I have been talking about our family projects. We have decided that in a couple of weeks, when we finish this unit, our classes will hold Family Day. Each of you may invite one or two members of your family to come to school for a program. We can show off what we have been learning. Also, we will play a game to see who comes to Family Day and try to guess who belongs with whom. That might be harder than it sounds."

Ms. Colman was smiling. I thought I knew why. First of all, we did not know the kids in Mr. Berger's class very well. We did not know who was in whose family. Then I thought about my own family. Would anyone guess that Emily was my sister? I remembered our talk about families. The kids in my class lived with parents, stepparents, grandparents, aunts, uncles, and foster families. Ms. Colman's game might be harder than it sounded.

Who would I bring to Family Day? Easy.

51

Mommy and Daddy. I love when we are together again. And I love spending extra time with Daddy.

"Now, class," Ms. Colman was saying, "think about Family Day. What kinds of things would you like to do with your families?"

"Eat!" cried Edwin. (He is from Mr. Berger's class.)

Ms. Colman smiled. "What can we do to show them what we have been learning these last few weeks?"

I raised my hand. "Show them our family trees," I said.

"Good idea," replied Ms. Colman. "We will display the family trees."

"We could tell them about animal families," suggested Chris.

"Another good idea," said Ms. Colman.

Edwin raised his hand and tried again. "Maybe we could read the stories and poems we are writing about families."

"Terrific," said Ms. Colman. "Now let's

think about who is going to do what. First of all, raise your hand if you have not finished your family tree yet."

We talked about Family Day projects for a long time. Finally Mr. Berger's kids returned to his room, and my classmates came back.

"Who are you going to invite to Family Day?" I asked Nancy and Hannie.

"Mommy and Sari," replied Hannie. (Sari is Hannie's little sister.)

Nancy frowned. "I'm not sure," she said. "I want to invite Mommy and Daddy. But if I do that, then Danny cannot come." (Danny is Nancy's new baby brother.) "If I invite — "

Nancy was interrupted by Audrey. " 'Scuse me," she said. She pulled me away from my friends. "Karen, Karen! I have to ask you something!" she exclaimed.

"What is it?"

"Will you be one of my guests at Family Day? After all, you are my twin."

"Audrey, I cannot be your guest at Family Day," I told her. "I am sorry, but I cannot. Anyway, I will be busy with my mother and father."

"Oh," said Audrey.

I hoped Audrey understood. Being twins was just a game. She knew that. Didn't she?

Hiding

"K aren," said Nancy one day. "Hannie and I never see you alone anymore."

"Never," echoed Hannie. "Not at school, anyway. You are always with Audrey." Hannie was whining. Nancy sounded whiney, too.

"Well, I cannot help that," I said. "Everywhere I go, she goes."

This was true. I had a shadow, and the shadow was named Audrey. I did not have any privacy. Once I stayed in the girls' room for fifteen whole minutes — just because Audrey was *not* there. I needed to be away from her for a little while. Another day, I kept hiding from her on the playground. Whenever I saw Audrey, I ran someplace else.

"Hannie," I said, "Nancy — "

"Hi, twin!" called Audrey.

"Hi!" I called back. Then I turned to my friends. "Meet me behind the big tree at recess today," I whispered. "We will try to hide from Audrey."

As soon as I finished my lunch that day, I ran to the playground.

Audrey was still inside, eating. I did not tell her where I was going. When I reached the tree, Nancy and Hannie were there.

"Hi, you guys!" I said. "We are alone at last."

"Not for long," said Hannie glumly. "I bet Audrey will be here any minute."

"You know what? We have not played together after school lately," I said. "Not just the three of us."

"That is because you have been too busy with Audrey," said Nancy.

"Well, let's play together today," I went on. "Can you come over to the little house this afternoon?"

Hannie and Nancy smiled. "Yes," they replied.

And just in time. The next thing I knew, Audrey was at my side.

That afternoon, the Three Musketeers sat in a row on my bed.

"I have a big problem," I announced. "Audrey is a gigundo pest. I have to do something. Will you guys help me?"

"Sure," said Hannie.

"Now let me see," said Nancy. "What could you do so Audrey will not want you to be her twin anymore?"

We sat and talked. By the time my friends went home, I was ready to put a plan into action. I would put it into action the next day.

Twin Trouble

This was my plan for twin trouble. It had been Nancy's idea mostly. "If Audrey wants to be your twin," she had said, "you should do everything together. *Every*thing," she added.

"But we already do!" I wailed.

Hannie had grinned at me. "Not *every*thing," she said.

"Oh," spoke up Nancy. "You mean *every*thing."

The next morning, I reached school before Audrey did. I sat patiently at my desk, my hands folded.

When Audrey arrived she ran straight to me.

"Hi, Karen!" she cried. "Guess what my dad told me."

"Hi, Karen!" I said. "Guess what my dad told me." I started talking just a couple of seconds after Audrey did. I repeated what she said while she was still finishing her sentence. Sam taught me that trick. It sounds hard to do, but it is not. It is easy. And it is very annoying. The last time I did it to David Michael he called me Princess Pest. Then he did not talk for three hours. To anybody.

But Audrey just stared at me. Her mouth dropped open. "How did you do that?" she asked. "That is amazing."

I started talking before Audrey was finished. "How did you do that?" I said. "That is amazing."

"Come on, Karen. Answer me."

"Come on, Karen. Answer me," I said.

"What is the matter with you? What are you doing?"

"What is the matter with you? What are you doing?"

Ms. Colman came into the room then, and everybody dashed for their seats. I think Audrey was glad to get away from me. But at lunchtime she sat next to me as usual.

I peeked into her bag, to see what she had brought for lunch.

"You know, Audrey," I said, "if we are going to be *real* twins, we should eat the same things for lunch. So we should divide everything we brought and each eat half of it."

Audrey looked at my sandwich. She wrinkled her nose. "But you have tuna fish," she said. "I do not want tuna."

Just in time I remembered to say, "But you have tuna fish. I do not want tuna." I wrinkled my nose. Then I handed Audrey half of the sandwich anyway.

"No, really. I mean it. I do not want tuna."

"No, really. I mean it. I do not want tuna."

"Karen!"

"Karen!

I gave Audrey half of my raisins and half of my orange, too. Then I pretended to think about something very hard. Finally I said, "Audrey, you know what? We did not get the same grade on our math quizzes. You got a ninety-five and I got an eighty-two. I think we should ask Ms. Colman to change your grade. You should have an eighty-two like me. Then we can be the same."

"No! That is not fair!" exclaimed Audrey.

"No! That is not fair!"

"Karen, stop!"

"Karen, stop!"

I did not stop. By the end of the day, Audrey looked very confused.

The Trouble With Emily

On Friday, Mommy drove Andrew and me to Daddy's house. It was another big-house weekend. At last.

"Kristy," I said to my big sister after dinner. "When are we going to have Adoption Day? When will we have the party for Emily?"

Kristy frowned. "I am not sure," she replied. "My mom and your dad are still having trouble with those papers. They are waiting for something important to come in the mail."

"Oh," I said. I was worried about Emily. Plus, I was feeling impatient. I wanted to start planning that party.

At bedtime I had to look for Elizabeth. Usually she comes to my room to tuck me in. But not that night. I think she had forgotten about me. Elizabeth was on the phone. She looked cross. She was saying, "But it *isn't* here, Peter. They sent the wrong form. . . . What? Tomorrow? Are you sure? . . . All right. The mail usually arrives after lunch."

Elizabeth saw me then. She held out her arm toward me. She kissed me good night, but she did not get off the phone.

On Saturday, Emily wanted to play dress-ups. We pulled the clothes out of the trunk in the playroom.

"What do you want to be, Emily?" I asked. "How about a cowgirl? Or a Lovely Lady? Or Batman?"

"Pea-cess," replied Emily. That meant "princess."

I helped Emily put on a gown and a crown. Then we found a magic wand for her. I led her downstairs.

"Elizabeth!" I called.

Elizabeth was standing by the front door. She looked cross again. "Where *is* it? Where *is* it?" she kept saying.

"Where is what?" I asked her.

"Oh, the mail," she replied.

"I pea-cess!" announced Emily.

Elizabeth did not even hear her. She exclaimed, "There it is!" She ran outside and across the lawn. She met the mail carrier just as he pulled his truck up to our box. I watched Mr. Venta hand her a stack of letters. Then Elizabeth ran back to the house. She shuffled through the envelopes. She ripped one open. Then she cried, "I don't believe it! They sent the wrong form *again*!"

Elizabeth flew to the phone in the kitchen. I stood in the hallway and tried to listen to her end of the conversation. But that was hard. Emily kept jumping around, shouting, "I pea-cess! I pea-cess!"

"Emily, shhh!" I said finally. I listened again. I heard Elizabeth say, " . . . have to go back." A moment later, I heard her say, "Oh, poor Emily." Then she added, "This is so hard."

My mouth hung open. I stared at my sister. Emily was dancing in circles in her pea-cess costume. How could we send her back to Vietnam? Even when Emily was being a gigundo pest I had not *really* wanted to get rid of her. I loved her.

"Emily," I said, "no matter what, you will not have to go back. I promise I will save you."

I scooped up Emily. I carried her to the stairs. Then I led her all the way up to the third floor. We hardly ever go there. If I hid Emily very carefully, no one would find her.

And that is what I did. I left Emily in the attic with a lot of toys and some crackers. I told her I would be back soon.

The Truth About Emily

When I went back downstairs, the first thing I heard was Nannie calling, "Emily! Naptime!"

Of course Emily did not answer her.

Nannie kept calling. Soon Daddy and Elizabeth were calling, too. Then Kristy and Charlie joined them. I pretended I did not know a thing about my little sister. "Emily! Emily!" I called.

Daddy looked panicky. "I will check outside," he said. Daddy checked outside. Kristy checked the basement. When they did not find her, Elizabeth said, "Okay, I am going to phone the police."

Uh-oh.

"Wait! Wait!" I cried. "Don't call the police!"

"Why not?" asked Daddy sharply.

"Well . . . because I know where Emily is. I hid her. She is in the attic."

Daddy gave me a Look. Then he ran upstairs. The rest of us ran after him. Sure enough, Emily was in the attic. She was looking at Lotto cards and eating a Saltine. "Hi, Daddy," she said.

Everyone hugged Emily. Then Nannie put her down for her nap, as if nothing had happened.

And then Daddy turned to me. "Karen," he said, "would you please tell us why you hid Emily in the attic?"

I was in the living room with the grown-ups. I was sitting on the couch between Daddy and Elizabeth. Nannie was in an armchair. "I put Emily there," I began, "because I thought if you could not find her, you could not send her back."

"Send her back?" repeated Elizabeth. "What do you mean?"

"*You* know," I said. "I heard you on the phone. Something is wrong with Emily's adoption. You said poor Emily will have to go back. I do not *want* her to go back to Vietnam. Even if she is a pest. I do not think that would be fair to Emily. I know I should not have hidden her. But please do not send her back."

"Oh, Karen," said all the grown-ups at the same time.

Then Elizabeth said, "Honey, Emily is not going to go anywhere. Yes, we are having a little trouble with some paperwork. But Emily is here to stay. No one has ever said she might have to go back to Vietnam. I think you misunderstood what you heard today. Someone sent us the wrong papers. They are not the ones we have been waiting for. I meant that I will have to send the *papers* back. That is all. And I said "poor Emily" because this is so frustrating. We just want her papers in order so that we do not have to worry about that anymore."

"Elizabeth? What is red tape?" I asked.

Elizabeth laughed. "Red tape. That is just an expression. It means lots of papers and procedures that use up time and do not seem necessary. But they have to be taken care of anyway."

"Oh," I said. "I have been looking for pieces of red tape!"

Daddy smiled. Then he said, "I know you were trying to help Emily when you hid her, Karen. But you do see that hiding her in the attic would not have solved any problems. Don't you?"

I nodded. "Yes. Daddy? When *are* we going to have Adoption Day?"

"As soon as the red tape is taken care of. Probably in about two weeks."

"Two weeks? Cool! We can start thinking about Emily's party."

I felt happy. I felt relieved. I felt so good that I changed my mind about something. I decided to invite Daddy and Emily to Family Day at school. Not Daddy and Mommy. Anyone could bring her parents. But I wanted my classmates to see what a wonderful and unusual family I have.

The Big Joke

I had noticed something. It seemed to me that Tammy and Terri looked more and more alike every day. First they just wore matching outfits. Then they began to fix their hair the same way. (They used to wear their hair differently, so we could always tell who was who.) Then they added matching jewelry. One day they came into Ms. Colman's room wearing brand-new flowered dresses. The dresses were exactly alike. On their feet were white knee socks and blue Mary Jane shoes. The *same* shoes. They had parted their hair on the left side, and put blue barrettes on the right side.

They wore gold necklaces, and tiny gold rings on their lefthand pinky fingers. They were even wearing the same watch on their left wrists.

"Hannie!" I whispered. "I cannot tell the twins apart!"

No one could.

The twins loved it. They teased us. One of them said, "I am Terri. I promise I am Terri. . . . Fooled you! I am Tammy."

I did not know if she was fooling or not.

After awhile, the twins pulled Nancy and Hannie and me into a corner. "Guess what," said one. "We are going to play a joke on everyone today. We are going to trade places. I bet we can even fool Ms. Colman and Mr. Berger. I am going to be Tammy, and Tammy will be me."

"You cannot do that!" I exclaimed.

"Oh, yes we can," said Terri. "No one will know."

"You mean you are going to go to Mr. Berger's room today, Tammy?" I asked. "And Terri will stay here?"

Tammy nodded. "Yup. And right now we are going to switch places for Ms. Colman. I will sit at Terri's desk, and she will sit at mine. Ms. Colman will never know."

Nancy frowned. "If we cannot tell you apart, how will we know you are really switching places?" she asked.

"Because I can prove I am Terri," said Terri. "Remember when I fell off my bike and had to get stitches in my knee?" (My friends and I nodded.) "Okay, there is the scar. So I am Terri."

Well, this was going to be a very interesting day.

When Ms. Colman came into the room, I watched the twins. Sure enough, Terri sat at Tammy's desk, and Tammy sat at Terri's.

Ms. Colman did not say a word. She let Chris take roll. Chris likes to call the names out loud. When he called Terri's name, Tammy said, "Here!" When he called Tammy's name, Terri said, "Here!"

Soon it was time to work with Mr. Berger's kids. I began to wonder about some things. How would Tammy be able to work on Terri's project on animal families? How would Terri be able to finish Tammy's poem about brothers and sisters? And how would Tammy know the rules in Mr. Berger's room? I bet they are different from Ms. Colman's rules.

I began to think the twin switch might not be a very good idea. My heart was pounding when Tammy walked into Mr. Berger's room. But nothing happened all morning. Ms. Colman called Terri "Tammy," and Terri answered. She finished Tammy's poem. Later, Tammy came back from Mr. Berger's room. She was holding Terri's project. It was all finished.

" 'Bye, Terri!" called Mr. Berger. "Nice work!"

" 'Bye!" replied Tammy.

I turned around and looked at Nancy and Hannie. My friends and I giggled. Then we watched Terri sit at Tammy's desk, and Tammy sit at Terri's desk. The twins had played a very big joke.

Pretend Sisters

All day, Tammy was Terri, and Terri was Tammy. They traded places during lunch and recess and in the afternoon. Then, about five minutes before the last bell of the day, Terri raised her hand.

"Yes, Tammy?" said Ms. Colman.

Terri grinned. "I am not Tammy," she said.

Ms. Colman looked confused. "Excuse me?"

"I am not Tammy. I am Terri," said Terri.

She stood up. Then she and Tammy switched seats.

"We fooled you all day!" exclaimed Tammy. "We fooled everybody! You and Mr. Berger and the teachers on the playground — and everybody!"

"Not me," I said.

"Well, no. Not Karen," agreed Tammy. "Or Hannie or Nancy. We told them what we were going to do. But we tricked everyone else."

Bobby Gianelli looked impressed. "Cool," he said.

Chris Lamar looked impressed, too. But then he said, "Prove it."

So Terri showed us the scar on her knee.

Ms. Colman laughed. "Girls," she said, "that was a wonderful trick. I don't know how you did it. But I do want to say one thing. I miss having Tammy and Terri in my class. Different girls I can tell apart. Dressing in matching outfits must be fun, but I like having two of you, not one of you."

The bell rang then. Ms. Colman assigned us a page in our science workbook for homework. Then my friends and I began to put away our things, and find our coats and hats and mittens. A lot of kids were talking to the twins. Some were saying congratulations.

But not Audrey. Audrey came over to my desk. She looked as if she wanted to cry.

"What is the matter?" I asked her.

"It's — it's Terri and Tammy," she replied. "It's what they did."

"Their joke?" I asked.

Audrey nodded. A tear rolled down her cheek. "Don't you see, Karen? We could never do what they did. We could never play a joke like that. Mr. Berger would just have said, 'Audrey, what are you doing in my room? And where is Karen?' He would never have thought I was you. No one would. No one *does*. I was silly to think we could be twins."

Good, I thought. Maybe Audrey would stop copying me. Maybe we would not

80

have to dress alike anymore. That would be fine with me. Still, I knew Audrey was feeling sad.

"I guess you are right," I said to her. "We are not twins. I am glad we can stop pretending. But not all twins look the same, you know. Some do and some do not. Some just look like sisters, or brothers, or sisters and brothers. So maybe we could be pretend sisters sometimes, Audrey. But just *pretend* sisters. And only sometimes."

Audrey smiled a little. "Pretend sisters?" she repeated. "That would be fine. I just don't want to be so lonely all the time."

"Why are you lonely?" I asked. "You have lots of friends at school."

"But not at home," she said. "No one lives near me. And now my brother is away at college. I miss him so much."

Oh, I thought. So that is why Audrey wanted a twin. Twins are never lonely. They always have each other. That is what Tammy and Terri say. And they should know.

"Well, *do* you want to be my pretend sister sometimes?" I asked Audrey.

She nodded. "A pretend sister is much, much better than no sister or brother at all. Thank you, Karen."

"You're welcome," I replied.

Family Day

"**H**ere they come! Here they come!" I cried.

"Indoor voice, Karen," said Ms. Colman.

"Here they come," I whispered.

It was Family Day at last. The kids in Ms. Colman's class and in Mr. Berger's class had been waiting for Family Day for a long time. We had put our poems and family trees on the bulletin boards. We had written a song about families. Now our two classrooms were ready for our guests. First the guests would come to Ms. Colman's room.

We would sing our song for them. Then we would try to figure out who is in whose family. We would know some people, of course, but not everyone. Then our guests would go to Mr. Berger's room for cookies and juice. (We baked the cookies ourselves.)

My classmates and I were crowded together at the front of our room. Mr. Berger's kids were with us. We watched as our first guests arrived.

"Do you know who they are?" Nancy whispered to me. An old woman and an old man were sitting down in the back of the classroom.

I shook my head. "The twins' grandparents?" I guessed. But I was not sure. I had not seen them before. Maybe they belonged to someone in Mr. Berger's room. Next a mom and dad came in. I waved to them. I knew who they were. Nancy's mother and father. Then I saw Mr. Simmons — Ms. Colman's husband.

Soon our guests began to arrive more

quickly. When Daddy and Emily entered the room, some of Mr. Berger's kids looked confused. "Who is she?" I heard one girl whisper. "Is that her father?"

When all of our guests were seated at the back of the room, us kids stood in four lines in the front. Mr. Berger stood before us. "Ready?" he whispered. "And one and two and *three*!"

My friends and I began our song. It was about how a family is like a patchwork quilt — the different pieces fit together, and there is always room to add more pieces. When the song was over, our guests clapped loudly.

Then our guessing game began. One by one our guests stepped forward. One guy looked about Charlie's age. He was wearing a sweat shirt with the words PRINCETON UNIVERSITY on the front. No one could guess who he was, so he said his name: Allen Green. He was Audrey's big brother. He was home from college for a long weekend.

A young woman holding a baby fooled us, too. She turned out to be Mr. Berger's wife with their little girl.

Boy, my friends have some interesting families. Edwin introduced us to his foster parents. Chris introduced us to his aunt and uncle. He said they are just like a mother and a father to him. And the twins introduced us to their grandparents. (They were the people I had noticed earlier.) At last Daddy and Emily stood up. Most of my classmates knew who they were, but nobody in Mr. Berger's class did. So I stepped over to them. "This is my father," I said. "And this is Emily Michelle Thomas Brewer. She is my adopted sister. Soon we are going to celebrate Adoption Day. We are going to have a party and a cake for Emily. I love my sister very much. You know — " I was going to tell everyone about the papers and the red tape and hiding Emily in the attic, but Ms. Colman was waving her hands at me. We had to finish

the guessing game. So I went back to my friends.

When the game was over, our guests wandered around. They ate the cookies and looked at our projects. I showed Daddy my family trees. "I was the only person who made two," I told him proudly. "And see? Andrew and I are on both trees. We are lucky, lucky, lucky."

Four Lovely Ladies

Family Day was over. It had been over for a week. And the old Audrey Green was back — the one who dressed the way *she* wanted, and colored her *own* pictures, and ate her lunch in whatever order *she* liked. She did not follow me around or wear silly fake glasses. She was even letting her bangs grow out. Audrey was through being my twin, and I was glad.

So were Nancy and Hannie.

"We can play together at recess," said Nancy. "We do not have to hide anymore."

"Just like old times," added Hannie.

I smiled at them. But I had not forgotten what I had said to Audrey. And one day I invited her over to play at the big house. "You are my pretend sister," I reminded her. "You better meet the rest of your pretend family."

Audrey came on a Saturday morning. Her mom dropped her off. She had said Audrey could stay for lunch. That was great. I decided to invite Hannie and Nancy over for a Lovely Ladies Luncheon.

When Audrey arrived, everyone in my big-house family was at home. I introduced Audrey to them. "This is Daddy, and this is Emily, and this is Andrew. You have already met them. Okay, and this is Elizabeth, my stepmother. And these are my stepbrothers, Charlie and Sam and David Michael. And this is my stepsister, Kristy. And this is Nannie."

Then I introduced Audrey to the pets. Audrey looked a little nervous. But she said, "This is the best patchwork family I have ever seen."

"We are a crazy quilt," said Sam, smiling.

Later, I showed Audrey my bedroom. We could hear Andrew and Emily building something with Lincoln Logs in the playroom. "You are never lonely here, are you?" said Audrey.

"Never," I agreed. "You know what? You can come to the big house any time you want company, Audrey. Except . . ."

"Except what?"

"Except I am not here very often. Only two weekends each month. I wish I could see Daddy and my big-house family more. But I cannot."

"Why?"

"I don't know. This is how Mommy and Daddy worked things out."

"Hi!" Emily burst into my room then. "I pea-cess," she cried.

"But Emily, you are wearing a pirate costume," I said.

Emily did not care.

Audrey and I played with Emily and Andrew for awhile. Then we ran outside and played in the snow. We were pulling each other around on a sled when Hannie and Nancy came over.

"Halloooo!" called Nancy. "We are here for the Lovely Ladies Luncheon!"

Audrey and I put away the sled. It was time to act like Lovely Ladies.

The four Lovely Ladies held their luncheon in the TV room. We sat on the floor around the coffee table. We ate peanut butter sandwiches and alphabet soup, but we pretended we were eating tea sandwiches and ladyfingers. "Lovely Ladies must always eat ladyfingers," said Hannie.

"Do you guys really want to be *ladies* when you grow up?" Audrey asked the Three Musketeers. She wrinkled her nose.

"No way," replied Hannie. "We just like to act like ladies now. When we grow up we want to have jobs."

"*And* be mothers," I added.

Nancy nodded.

"Oh, good," said Audrey. "I was hoping you would say that."

After our luncheon we went outside again. We built a fort and had a snowball fight. When Audrey had to leave, Nancy and Hannie and I called, " 'Bye! See you in school on Monday! Come back soon!"

Adoption Day

One evening I was in my room at the little house. I was playing with Emily Junior and writing a poem about her. I was going to call the poem "Ode to a Rat." All I had written so far was "Ratty, dear ratty."

I heard the telephone ring. Then I heard Seth call, "Karen! Andrew! Please come to the phone! Your father wants to talk to you."

Andrew picked up the phone in the kitchen. I picked up the phone in Mommy and Seth's room. "Good news, kids,"

Daddy said to us. "Emily's papers are signed and finished and in order."

"You mean you got through the red tape?" I asked.

"That's right," replied Daddy. "And Adoption Day is going to be on Saturday, when you two are here. Get ready for a party!"

I was very busy after that phone call. So was Andrew. We decided to make presents for Emily. Andrew wanted to build a truck for her out of Legos. I let him do that, but I started on something I hoped she would want to keep forever. A book for Emily.

I found photos of Emily and glued them onto the pages of her book. I glued down photos of Daddy and Kristy and everyone in the big house, too. I wanted to show Emily how she fit into our patchwork family. I wrote a poem for Emily. Andrew told me everything he remembered about the day Daddy and Elizabeth brought Emily home. I wrote his words down for him.

Then I made a cover for the book. I called the book *The Story of Emily*. Under the title I wrote "By Karen Brewer With Some Help From Andrew Brewer."

Andrew and I wrapped the book together.

A week and a half went by. On Saturday morning I woke up at the big house. It was Adoption Day.

I leaped out of bed. I ran downstairs. Emily's party was going to start at two o'clock. We had a lot to do.

"Morning, Nannie!" I cried as I ran into the kitchen.

"Morning, sweetie," said Nannie.

I think Nannie had been up for awhile. She was putting a cake in the oven. She had already baked a batch of lemon bars. I pitched in and helped her. (I am not a bad cook.)

That morning my big-house family and I cooked and cleaned and wrapped presents. Twice, Charlie had to run to the store to buy last-minute things. I went with him. I like riding in his car, the Junk Bucket.

At two o'clock our doorbell began to ring. The Papadakises came over. So did Nancy and her family. So did Kristy's friends and lots of Daddy and Elizabeth's grown-up friends. Nannie's bowling team even came to the party.

Everyone brought presents for Emily.

"My birfday?" she kept asking. "I two? I fee?" I tried to explain things to her. "Not your birthday, Emily," I said. "Even better. This is Adoption Day. Not many people get to have a birthday *and* Adoption Day. This means you are *officially* part of our family now. It means you and I are really and truly sisters."

"Emily, come open your presents," called Daddy.

Emily opened presents forever. (Daddy said he would read *The Story of Emily* to her at bedtime.) Then Nannie and Charlie brought in her Adoption Day cake. No candles were on it, but Daddy and Elizabeth

began to sing a song to the tune of "Happy Birthday."

"Happy adoption to you!" they sang. Everyone else joined in. "Happy adoption to you! Happy adoption, dear Emily! Happy adoption to you!"

Emily smiled. I hoped Adoption Day would be one of the happiest days of her life.

About the Author

ANN M. MARTIN lives in New York City and loves animals, especially cats. She has two cats of her own, Mouse and Rosie.

Other books by Ann M. Martin that you might enjoy are *Stage Fright; Me and Katie (the Pest)*; and the books in *The Baby-sitters Club* series.

Ann likes ice cream and *I Love Lucy*. And she has her own little sister, whose name is Jane.

Little Sister

Don't miss #46

KAREN'S BABY-SITTER

Mommy led Bart into the kitchen. "Here is the number of the office where you can reach Mr. Engle and me. Here is the number of the children's doctor. And here are other emergency numbers. Now don't let the kids eat too much, okay? Mr. Engle and I will be home by six, and we will give the kids dinner then."

"Okay," said Bart.

I could not wait for Mommy to leave. Even though the weather was yucky and we would have to stay inside, I knew we would have fun.

I was right. Bart let us do anything we wanted to do.

B·A·B·Y S·I·T·T·E·R·S

Little Sister™

by Ann M. Martin, author of *The Baby-sitters Club* ®

☐	MQ44300-3 #1	Karen's Witch	$2.75
☐	MQ44259-7 #2	Karen's Roller Skates	$2.75
☐	MQ44299-7 #3	Karen's Worst Day	$2.75
☐	MQ44264-3 #4	Karen's Kittycat Club	$2.75
☐	MQ44258-9 #5	Karen's School Picture	$2.75
☐	MQ44298-8 #6	Karen's Little Sister	$2.75
☐	MQ44257-0 #7	Karen's Birthday	$2.75
☐	MQ42670-2 #8	Karen's Haircut	$2.75
☐	MQ43652-X #9	Karen's Sleepover	$2.75
☐	MQ43651-1 #10	Karen's Grandmothers	$2.75
☐	MQ43650-3 #11	Karen's Prize	$2.75
☐	MQ43649-X #12	Karen's Ghost	$2.95
☐	MQ43648-1 #13	Karen's Surprise	$2.75
☐	MQ43646-5 #14	Karen's New Year	$2.75
☐	MQ43645-7 #15	Karen's in Love	$2.75
☐	MQ43644-9 #16	Karen's Goldfish	$2.75
☐	MQ43643-0 #17	Karen's Brothers	$2.75
☐	MQ43642-2 #18	Karen's Home-Run	$2.75
☐	MQ43641-4 #19	Karen's Good-Bye	$2.95
☐	MQ44823-4 #20	Karen's Carnival	$2.75
☐	MQ44824-2 #21	Karen's New Teacher	$2.95
☐	MQ44833-1 #22	Karen's Little Witch	$2.95
☐	MQ44832-3 #23	Karen's Doll	$2.95

More Titles... ➡

██

The Baby-sitters Little Sister titles continued...

☐ MQ44859-5	#24	Karen's School Trip	$2.75
☐ MQ44831-5	#25	Karen's Pen Pal	$2.75
☐ MQ44830-7	#26	Karen's Ducklings	$2.75
☐ MQ44829-3	#27	Karen's Big Joke	$2.75
☐ MQ44828-5	#28	Karen's Tea Party	$2.75
☐ MQ44825-0	#29	Karen's Cartwheel	$2.75
☐ MQ45645-8	#30	Karen's Kittens	$2.75
☐ MQ45646-6	#31	Karen's Bully	$2.95
☐ MQ45647-4	#32	Karen's Pumpkin Patch	$2.95
☐ MQ45648-2	#33	Karen's Secret	$2.95
☐ MQ45650-4	#34	Karen's Snow Day	$2.95
☐ MQ45652-0	#35	Karen's Doll Hospital	$2.95
☐ MQ45651-2	#36	Karen's New Friend	$2.95
☐ MQ45653-9	#37	Karen's Tuba	$2.95
☐ MQ45655-5	#38	Karen's Big Lie	$2.95
☐ MQ43647-3		Karen's Wish Super Special #1	$2.95
☐ MQ44834-X		Karen's Plane Trip Super Special #2	$3.25
☐ MQ44827-7		Karen's Mystery Super Special #3	$2.95
☐ MQ45644-X		Karen's Three Musketeers Super Special #4	$2.95
☐ MQ45649-0		Karen's Baby Super Special #5	$3.25

Available wherever you buy books, or use this order form.

Scholastic Inc., P.O. Box 7502, 2931 E. McCarty Street, Jefferson City, MO 65102

Please send me the books I have checked above. I am enclosing $ _____
(please add $2.00 to cover shipping and handling). Send check or money order - no cash
or C.O.Ds please.

Name _____

Address _____

City _____ State/Zip _____

Please allow four to six weeks for delivery. Offer good in U.S.A. only. Sorry, mail orders are not
available to residents to Canada. Prices subject to change.   BLS1092

██

NOW PLAYING!

THE BABY-SITTERS CLUB

Home Video Collection

Look for these all new episodes!

■

Claudia and the Mystery of the Secret Passage

Dawn Saves the Trees

The Baby-sitters and the Boy Sitters

Jessi and the Mystery of the Stolen Secrets

Stacey Takes a Stand

The Baby-sitters Remember

■

Available wherever fun videos are sold.

For More Information Call: 1-800-628-3100